CHRISTOPHER PUMPKIN

For Wanda, who likes all things fun —SH & PL

For Jon E, a spooky goth at heart —NE

Little, Brown and Company • Hachette Book Group • 1290 Avenue of the Americas, New York, NY 10104 • Visit us at LBYR.com • Originally published in 2019 by Hodder and Stoughton in Great Britain • First U.S. Hardcover Edition: July 2020 • Little, Brown and Company is a division of Hachette Book Group, Inc. •The Little, Brown name and logo are trademarks of Hachette Book Group, Inc. • The publisher is not responsible for websites (or their content) that are not owned by the publisher. • Library of Congress Cataloging-in-Publication Data • Names: Hendra, Sue, author. | Linnet, Paul, author. | East, Nick, illustrator. • Title: Christopher Pumpkin / written by Sue Hendra and Paul Linnet ; illustrated by Nick East. • Description: First U.S. edition. | New York : Little, Brown and Company, 2020. | Audience: Ages 4–8. | Summary: A witch enchants pumpkins to help with the huge, scary party she is throwing but fun-loving Christopher will have to embrace his differences in order to prove he can be frightening, too. • Identifiers: LCCN 2019053896 | ISBN 9780316427555 (hardcover) | ISBN 9780316427579 (ebook) | ISBN 9780316427548 (ebook other) • Subjects: CYAC: Stories in rhyme. | Pumpkins—Fiction. | Witches—Fiction. | Parties—Fiction. | Humorous stories. • Classification: LCC PZ8.3.H4148 Chr 2020 | DDC [E]—dc23 • LC record available at https://lccn.loc.gov/2019053896 • PRINTED IN CHINA • ISBNs: 978-0-316-42755-5 (hardcover), 978-0-316-42756-2 (board) • DC • 10 9 8 7 6 5 4 3 2 1

CHRISTOPHER PUMPKIN

Written by
Sue Hendra
and **Paul Linnet**

Illustrated by
Nick East

Little, Brown and Company
New York Boston

On Snaggletooth Lane in spooky Spooksville
was a dark, creepy castle, perched high on a hill.

Deep in that castle, by the glow of the fire,
sat a wicked old witch with a burning desire:
to throw a huge party, the scariest yet—
one that her friends would never forget.

SCARY
PARTY
TOMORROW

"There's too much to do! It'll drive me berserk!
Now, who can I find that will do all the work?"

She looked all around—then what did she spy?
A big pile of pumpkins she'd bought for a pie.

"THEY could be useful and scary as well.
I'll bring them to life with the help of a spell. . . ."

She was making an army and having a ball.
As they sprang into life she gave names to them all.

"Gnarly,

Grizzly,

Grunty,

Roar,

Snaggletooth,

Stink Face,

and maybe one more. . . ."

The witch raised her wand for one final go.
There were SPARKLES and GLITTER, then a voice said . . .

Hello!
I'm Christopher Pumpkin.
I like all things fun.
I'm SO happy to be here.
Group hug, everyone?

He stretched out his arms and gave them a grin,
overflowing with kindness and warmth from within.

"OH NO!" screeched the witch. "What on earth did I make?
You're supposed to be scary. I've made a mistake!"

"Now, hang on a minute," said Christopher P.
"I'm sure I'll fit in. Just wait and you'll see."

"All right," snapped the witch, "as there's so much to do, but, Christopher Pumpkin . . . I'll be watching you!"

FIZZZ CRACKLE

"Now, get on with your work and make decorations. I want horrible, ghastly, frightful creations."

"Did someone say decor? That's right up my street! Forget about tricks and prepare for a treat!"

There was lifting and shifting and huffing and grunting,
but while others hung cobwebs, Chris hung up bunting!

Then along came the witch. "Work harder, buffoons!"
But instead of bat lanterns, Chris chose balloons!

The horrified pumpkins all scuttled away.
They needed to find party music to play.

"My favorite music is howling and screaming,"
said Gnarly the Pumpkin, his scary eyes gleaming.

"I'm sorry," said Chris, "but that sounds bizarre. Let's all have a sing-song. I've brought my guitar."

Now for the food—it was time to begin,
so they stood around the cauldron, tossing things in.

GLUG GLUG

First some earwax, then hair from a yeti,
a poisonous bug, and some moldy spaghetti.

The result was rat pizza, all sprouting with hair
and stinky green cheese made from old underwear,

some hot curried slugs, fried spicy snakes . . .

. . . then in walked our Chris with some pink fairy cakes!

"This just isn't working! I think you'll agree,"
said the witch as she glared down at Christopher P.

"I've had quite enough. You're not part of this group.
If you can't be scary, I'll turn you to soup!

You've got till the morning. Have I made myself clear?"
Poor Christopher nodded, frozen with fear.

"I don't want to be soup, or a pie, or a stew.
I'll stay up all night and plan what to do.

I'm Christopher Pumpkin. I like all things fun.
But there must be a way I can scare everyone."

He worked through the night, never taking a break.
But the clock, it was ticking.
Soon the witch would awake!

SCRIBBLE
SCRIBBLE

SNORE

The morning arrived and the pumpkins all stared
at Christopher's bed. "He's gone!" they declared.

"I suppose that it's better he went without fuss.
There was really no chance he could ever scare US!"

Along came the witch. "Now out of my way,
my guests are arriving. The party's today!"

So poor Chris had vanished, or so it would seem,
but then from outside came an almighty . . .

There were unicorns skipping, balloons on the door,
fluffy pink kittens, and sparkles galore!

There were marshmallow puffs piled up in mountains.
Strawberry milkshake was squirting from fountains.

"I'm Christopher Pumpkin. I like all things fun."
But before he could finish, the witch shouted . . .

Wait!
Don't you like it?

Chris called
with delight . . .

"Well, one thing's for sure ... I scared **them** all right!"

SEP   2020

SEP   2020